Teen Activism LIBRARY

STAND UP
for Human Rights

Stephanie Lundquist-Arora

San Diego, CA

© 2022 ReferencePoint Press, Inc.
Printed in the United States

For more information, contact:
ReferencePoint Press, Inc.
PO Box 27779
San Diego, CA 92198
www.ReferencePointPress.com

ALL RIGHTS RESERVED.
No part of this work covered by the copyright hereon may be reproduced or used in any form or by any means—graphic, electronic, or mechanical, including photocopying, recording, taping, web distribution, or information storage retrieval systems—without the written permission of the publisher.

LIBRARY OF CONGRESS CATALOGING-IN-PUBLICATION DATA

Names: Lundquist-Arora, Stephanie, author.
Title: Stand up for human rights / Stephanie Lundquist-Arora.
Description: San Diego : ReferencePoint Press, 2021. | Series: Teen activism library | Includes bibliographical references and index.
Identifiers: LCCN 2021006842 (print) | LCCN 2021006843 (ebook) | ISBN 9781678201500 (library binding) | ISBN 9781678201517 (ebook)
Subjects: LCSH: Youth--Political activity--Juvenile literature. | Human rights workers--Juvenile literature.
Classification: LCC HQ799.2.P6 L86 2021 (print) | LCC HQ799.2.P6 (ebook) | DDC 320.0835/0973--dc23
LC record available at https://lccn.loc.gov/2021006842
LC ebook record available at https://lccn.loc.gov/2021006843

CONTENTS

Introduction   4
Young People for Human Rights

Chapter One   8
The Issue Is Human Rights

Chapter Two   19
The Activists

Chapter Three   31
The Teen Activist's Tool Kit

Chapter Four   42
Risks and Rights

Source Notes   53
Where to Go for Ideas and Inspiration   56
Index   59
Picture Credits   63
About the Author   64

INTRODUCTION

Young People for Human Rights

On January 8, 2021 Boko Haram killed fourteen people in Mozogo, Cameroon, the northern region of the West African country. Boko Haram is a jihadist movement that was formed in 2002. Its goals are to educate children in Islamic (rather than Western) schools and to create an Islamic state. Its tactics are notoriously violent, usually including abductions, bombings, and assassinations. When residents of Mozogo heard that Boko Haram was on the way to stage an attack, they ran to the nearby forest for safety. A suicide bomber who was already there hid among them and detonated explosives that killed eleven civilians. Boko Haram gunmen shot three other people from Mozogo during the attack.

Many of the terrorist group's victims are children and other vulnerable populations. In April 2020, for example, Boko Haram attacked a camp hosting eight hundred internally displaced people in the Far North region of Cameroon. During the attack, nineteen people died (including two suicide bombers), and sixteen were injured. The United Nations High Commissioner for Refugees (UNHCR), the United Nation's (UN) refugee agency, strongly condemned the attack. According to the UNHCR, Boko Haram's operations have affected approximately 26 million people in the Lake Chad region of Africa, which includes northern Cameroon, and displaced 2.6 million others. In October

2020 Voice of America—an international broadcaster funded by the US government—further reported that Cameroon had closed more than 60 schools on the northern border to protect children, teachers, and staff from continuing Boko Haram attacks.

A Grassroots Movement

Divina Maloum, born and raised in Cameroon, began advocating for the rights of people afflicted by terrorist groups like Boko Haram in her country. Maloum, now sixteen, began a grassroots youth-led movement called Children for Peace as a ten-year-old visiting her family in the northern part of Cameroon. There she had witnessed many human rights violations. She was disturbed by the effects of extreme messages and terrorism in the northern region. Children in conflict areas sometimes lose their lives or are injured, witness their parents being killed, and watch as their villages are consumed by flames and left to ashes. Terrorist groups target children in vulnerable situations forcing them to become brides, soldiers, or even sex slaves. Some children are recruited as suicide bombers to carry out attacks in crowded places such as markets, schools, churches, or refugee camps.

To stand up for human rights, in 2015 Maloum created Children for Peace, an organization that aims to increase children's participation in peace building and advocating for children's rights and gender equality. She believes that including children in the peace process will lead to a brighter future. In an interview in 2020 with Women Deliver, a global organization that promotes gender equality and the health and rights of girls and women, Maloum stated, "I believe that children should not be overlooked. If we have more children in peacebuilding, we will have fewer conflicts in the long-term."[1]

> "I believe that children should not be overlooked. If we have more children in peacebuilding, we will have fewer conflicts in the long-term."[1]
>
> —Divina Maloum, founder and leader of Children for Peace

Divina Maloum started a youth-led movement called Children for Peace at the age of ten after witnessing human rights violations while visiting her family in northern Cameroon. In 2019 Divina was awarded the Children's Peace Prize by human rights activist Bishop Desmond Tutu.

Together with one hundred permanent members of her growing organization, Maloum continues to spread national messages of peace and human rights. She has established peace advocacy groups in mosques and discusses peace and human rights with children in local communities. With some of these other children, Maloum further has created a children's declaration against violent extremism. She also warns Cameroon's children not to get involved in violence through the cartoons that she draws. For example, in one of her cartoons she has illustrated a scene in which a young girl refuses to accept a vest containing explosives. The caption reads, "I'm not a hero when I carry bombs."[2]

Aside from awareness raising, Maloum's messages of peace have also had an effect on reducing drug use in the local community. Her civic education teacher, Ntigang Oumarou, told Voice of America that as a result of Children for Peace's talks, which include discussions about children's use of drugs and alcohol, the police in Cameroon now work to ensure that alcohol and drugs are not sold in or around schools to children.

Maloum's efforts are effective and are not going unnoticed. In 2019 human rights activist Archbishop Desmond Tutu awarded her the International Children's Peace Prize. In her acceptance speech at The Hague, home to the International Court of Justice, Maloum said, "I invite my fellow children around the world to stand up for their rights."[3]

Young People Stand Against Injustice

Many young people are standing up for their rights and against injustice. There are myriad stories of teen activism that begin like Maloum's. They experience, witness, or learn about something they think is not right in real life or in the media, and they are compelled to act. Teens and children have made a difference campaigning for human rights by starting movements, raising awareness, protesting, writing to politicians, and even testifying in front of national governing bodies.

The first step for human rights activism is education. In order to be an advocate of one's own or others' rights, there must be an understanding of what those rights entail and what constitutes an injustice. According to Salil Shetty, former secretary-general of the human rights advocacy organization Amnesty International, "Human rights education is key to addressing the underlying causes of injustice around the world. The more people know about their rights, and the rights of others in society, the better equipped they are to protect them."[4]

> "Human rights education is key to addressing the underlying causes of injustice around the world. The more people know about their rights, and the rights of others in society, the better equipped they are to protect them."[4]
>
> —Salil Shetty, former secretary-general of Amnesty International

CHAPTER ONE

The Issue Is Human Rights

Torture of anyone, including prisoners, is a violation of human rights. Human rights are the basic freedoms and entitlements that all people deserve because they are humans. They transcend all identity categories (including political belief, race, religion, gender, sexual orientation, ethnicity, and economic class).

Human rights advocates believe that basic rights, like freedom from torture, should never be revoked or suspended. Human rights doctrine is deeply rooted in moral philosophy and made explicit in the Universal Declaration of Human Rights (UDHR). The UDHR, proclaimed by the UN General Assembly in Paris on December 10, 1948, is the common standard for universal human rights and the foundation for international law governing human rights. International human rights law is based on a system of treaties, international laws, and domestic laws. In its preamble and thirty articles, the UDHR includes the right to liberty, life, freedom, safety, property, and marriage equality. It is meant to protect individuals and groups from many incursions. Most of these rights seem clear until a situation arises that blurs the line—such as when governments use harsh tactics to maintain order.

Torture in Syrian Prisons

Systemic torture in prisons is one of the main tools that the Syrian government, led by President Bashar al-Assad, uses to deter dissent. For the infraction of peaceful protest, Muhannad Ghabbash was a victim of torture under the Syrian government for nineteen months. Ghabbash, a law student, began organizing protests in Aleppo in 2011 at age twenty-two. He was arrested and detained for the first time in June of that year for demonstrating against the government. Because it was his first offense, he was released, but only after he promised to not protest again. Two months later he was arrested again for protesting—and was beaten. This time he was told to leave the country. He did not leave, nor did he stop protesting against government injustices.

The third time Ghabbash was arrested for peaceful protest, he nearly paid with his life. Syrian government forces tortured a confession out of him for planning a bombing, a crime he did not commit. They hung him by his wrists, beat him, shocked him with electricity, and held him at gunpoint. Sometimes they put him in a tire and beat him until he passed out, only to wake up naked in a cold hallway to be beaten again. One time they told him a woman screaming out of sight was his mother, a form of psychological torture. Eventually, they broke his will, and he confessed to a crime he did not commit. After fleeing to Turkey, Ghabbash was interviewed by the *New York Times*. He told the interviewer, "I don't want to confess something I haven't done. Five people asking questions at once. You're cold, you're thirsty, lips full of blood, you can't focus. Everybody is screaming, hitting."[5]

> "I don't want to confess something I haven't done. Five people asking questions at once. You're cold, you're thirsty, lips full of blood, you can't focus. Everybody is screaming, hitting."[5]
>
> —Muhannad Ghabbash, victim of torture in Syria

Ghabbash's inhumane treatment did not end after his confession, for which his sentence was death. He endured daily beatings. One of the prison guards, who called himself Hitler, further organized dinners for his colleagues during which inhumane treatment and torture of the prisoners, including Ghabbash, was the entertainment. Prisoners were used as the tables and chairs for the attendees. Other prisoners were hung from fences and made to refer to the guards as master and beg for water sprayed from a hose. Prisoners were further required to act as animals and show jealousy if the guard called Hitler showed attention to the other prisoners. After nearly two years under these conditions, Ghabbash's freedom was purchased with the bribing of a judge, a common practice in Syria. Many other prisoners did not survive. According to the Syrian Network for Human Rights, more than fourteen thousand prisoners have been tortured and killed in Syria since the civil war began there in 2011.

Human Rights Organizations Condemn Torture

The Syrian government is violating fundamental human rights with its torture of prisoners. Pro-government forces are trying to quash a decade-long rebellion with whatever means they have.

Gathered at the Turkish border during the Arab Spring uprisings in 2011, Syrian refugees protest the harsh tactics their government uses for maintaining order.

Unreasonable Detainment Violates Basic Human Rights

Human rights advocates argue that the detention of asylum seekers is a violation of the basic right to liberty. Waves of asylum seekers, many fleeing from persecution, have arrived at the US border since 2015. Under the Trump administration, US policy was to detain asylum seekers, sometimes separating children from their parents for indeterminate amounts of time and in inadequate conditions. Supporters of these practices defend their policies as a necessary means to analyze cases, deter people with false claims for asylum, and guard national security.

Michael Wangai (not his real name), a lawyer from Kenya, experienced immigration detention. After reporting bribery and corruption within his political party, Wangai's life was in danger. Two other witnesses had already been killed. Wangai knew that if he did not leave, he would be next. He took a flight to Tijuana, Mexico, where he applied for asylum at the US border. In August 2019, for the first few days of processing, Wangai was detained in a room that was 51°F (10.6°C) and slept on the floor with a foil blanket. After detention in multiple facilities for over a year, Wangai was denied asylum—a decision he is currently appealing. The immigration judge contended that because the members of his own political party were posing the threat, it was a personal matter.

When the line is blurred, activists rise up from both inside and outside of such circumstances to protect basic human rights where they are at risk.

For example, the Office of the United Nations High Commissioner for Human Rights, the UN's human rights office, has condemned the Iranian government's execution of Mohammad Hassan Rezaiee on December 31, 2020. Rezaiee was arrested in 2007 at age sixteen for allegedly stabbing a man to death. The evidence for his conviction was based on a confession extracted with torture. Rezaiee's execution, following twelve years on death row, was therefore a violation of human rights on two fronts. First, he was tortured to force his confession. And second, human rights advocates from Amnesty International contend that the execution of people for crimes they committed when they were children is "an abhorrent assault on children's rights."[6]

Human rights advocates from several organizations around the world also condemned the United States' use of torture for information at military prisons, such as Guantanamo Bay, following the September 11, 2001, terrorist attacks. One of the detainees, Khalid Shaikh Mohammed, was waterboarded 183 times in March 2003. Detainees were also subjected to sleep deprivation, as well as being put into coffin-sized boxes and slammed into walls for information-gathering purposes. Overseeing the torture tactics was James Mitchell, a former contract psychologist for the Central Intelligence Agency. Mitchell had no regrets regarding the techniques used during this time period. In January 2020, at the death penalty trial for five of the conspirators in the 9/11 terrorist attacks, Mitchell said, "I'd get up today and do it again. I thought my moral duty to protect American lives outweighed the feelings of discomfort of terrorists who voluntarily took up arms against us. To me it just seemed like it would be dereliction of my moral responsibilities."[7]

> "I thought my moral duty to protect American lives outweighed the feelings of discomfort of terrorists who voluntarily took up arms against us."[7]
>
> —James Mitchell, former contract psychologist for the Central Intelligence Agency

Waterboarding, the practice of simulating drowning by placing a cloth over a detainee's face and pouring water over him or her, is considered torture by human rights organizations. Many human rights advocates, including UN special rapporteur on torture Nils Melzer, appealed to the US government to end its practice of waterboarding. Melzer argues, "Torture is known to consistently produce false confessions and unreliable or misleading information. Faced with the imminent threat of excruciating pain or anguish, victims simply will say anything—regardless of whether it is true—to make the pain stop and try to stay alive."[8]

Acid Attacks

In addition to the purpose of extracting information, torture is also used as punishment, sometimes within a family. Acid

American soldiers escort a detainee to be interrogated by military officials at the US Naval Base at Guantanamo Bay, Cuba. Human rights advocates around the world have condemned the use of torture by American interrogators to obtain information.

attacks, in particular, occur when a person throws acid or a corrosive substance at another person to torture, permanently scar, or kill them. ActionAid, an international charity that works with women and girls living in poverty, estimates that there are fifteen hundred acid attacks globally per year. Many of these attacks are not reported. Most of them occur in India, Pakistan, and Bangladesh as a penalty to women and girls for refusing marriage or sex. The assailant usually aims for the victim's face for the purposes of public shame and visible disfigurement, affecting her ability to get married or gain employment in the future.

When Laxmi Agarwal was fifteen years old, she refused to marry thirty-two-year-old Nadeem Khan. While she was waiting

Sex Trafficking in the United States

Tonya was thirteen years old when she first met Eddie, an adult living in the same Dallas, Texas, apartment complex as her family. "Tonya" and "Eddie" are not their real names, but Tonya's story is real. At first there was flirting, but then their relationship developed into something more.

When Tonya was fifteen, she ran away from home and began living with Eddie. At first, Tonya cooked, cleaned, and looked after Eddie's children. She believed that she was in love with him. One night during a party, Tonya explains, "[Eddie] approached me and told me in so many words, 'I want you to have sex with this guy for money.' . . . He kept telling me, 'If you love me, you'll do this.'" Afterward, Eddie began advertising Tonya to potential customers. Tonya did as she was told; she felt she had no choice. Forced sex with strangers in hotel rooms became a daily occurrence for her. Eddie was eventually arrested and sentenced to twelve years in prison.

Tonya's story is not unique. The US Department of State estimates that 14,500 to 17,500 people are trafficked in the United States each year. Runaways are especially vulnerable. One out of seven reported missing are likely sex trafficking victims, according to the National Center for Missing and Exploited Children.

"Human Trafficking Victim Shares Her Story," U.S. Immigration and Customs Enforcement, February 10, 2021. https://www.ice.gov/features/human-trafficking-victim-shares-story.

---

for a bus in Delhi, India, Khan and his younger brother's girlfriend, Rakhi, threw acid at Agarwal's face and body in retaliation. The attack, for which Agarwal underwent seven surgeries, caused her serious physical pain and mental anguish. Agarwal tweets, "I felt as if someone had set my whole body on fire."[9]

In an uncommon move and with the support of her family, Agarwal decided to take the assailants to court. After four years, the court sentenced Khan to ten years in prison and Rakhi to seven years. This case marked the first time that an acid attack perpetrator was issued such a long sentence, setting an important precedent for future cases in India. Agarwal later founded the Chhanv Foundation, through

> "I felt as if someone had set my whole body on fire."[9]
>
> —Laxmi Agarwal, acid attack survivor

which she helps acid attack survivors with treatment, legal aid, and rehabilitation. Acid attacks, forced marriages, and child marriages are all in violation of human rights. Because of advocates like Agarwal, more of the acid attack assailants are being held accountable.

Child Marriages

In addition to acid attacks, where the victims are mostly women and girls, there are many other gender-based human rights violations. Sometimes, young girls are married off to adult men. Girls Not Brides, a global partnership with the mission of ending child marriage, reports that each year, 12 million girls are forced to marry before they are eighteen years old. Child marriages often subject girls to abuse, lead to early pregnancy, and decrease the likelihood that they will get a formal education. Human rights advocates contend that child marriages violate the rights to freedom, liberty, safety, and education.

Niger, a country in western Africa, has the highest rate of child marriages in the world. Almost 80 percent of girls there are married before they are eighteen years old. One of them, Hadiza (a false name used to protect her identity), was married against her will at age fourteen. Her father's younger brother had arranged her marriage to an older man in order to pay off a debt. Having no other way to pay what he owed, he offered his young niece's hand in marriage. Hadiza objected and ran away. After three days, a fisher found her exhausted in the woods, and her brother took her home. She ended up marrying the man to avoid bringing shame and misfortune on her family. Hadiza's husband forced her to quit school and moved her 620 miles (1,000 km) away from her family. He raped and beat her. She recounts, "The day that he took my virginity . . . he was accompanied by his four friends. They held me down as he took my virginity from me."[10]

Following three years of marriage, during which Hadiza gave birth to a stillborn baby and a second baby who lived, she was

Married against her will at eleven years old, a child bride in Niger stands in her bedroom. Nearly 80 percent of girls are married before the age of eighteen in Niger, which has the highest rate of child marriages in the world.

able to escape the abusive situation. She ran away to live with her maternal uncle. Hadiza subsequently finished high school, attained a professional diploma in electronics, and works for organizations that help young women in Niger.

Honor Killings

Honor killings are further in violation of a woman's basic rights to life, freedom, liberty and safety. In some cultures, people believe that the honor of a family is maintained through the good virtue of the women in it. The family's standing in the community is tied to the women's obedience to familial and social expectations. Family members in these cultures sometimes murder women for bringing perceived shame upon the family.

An example of this took place on May 14, 2020, in Pakistan's North Waziristan District. Earlier that month, a video from the year before was posted on social media. It showed two women, ages twenty-two and twenty-four, kissing a twenty-eight-year-old man on the lips. Members of their families decided they were honor bound to kill the women. The father of one of the victims and the brother of another subsequently were arrested and confessed to shooting and burying the women. Police also arrested the man in the video on the grounds of vulgarity. In 2016 Pakistan passed legislation in which honor killings were made illegal, with the penalty of life in prison. Prior to 2016 assailants were able to avoid the penalty for murder if the victim's family forgave them. While formal political achievements, like the ban on honor killings, are important, they are usually not enough to end human rights injustices. According to a 2019 report from Human Rights Watch, an independent human rights advocacy organization, there are an estimated one thousand honor killings each year in Pakistan.

Female Genital Mutilation

In certain cultures, predominantly but not exclusively in sub-Saharan Africa and Arab states, some people believe a way to maintain the virtue of a woman, and therefore the honor of her family, is to control her libido. In order to do this, part or all of a woman's external genitalia is removed, commonly referred to by human rights advocates as female genital mutilation (FGM). FGM is also practiced because it is a norm. In cultures where FGM is common, women with uncut genitalia often are regarded as unmarriable, because they are seen as unhealthy and impure. The procedure is dangerous, is painful, carries no health benefits, and causes many long-term problems. Problems might include but are not limited to the following: death from infection, painful intercourse, no sexual desire, irregular periods, bladder problems, recurrent infections, and complications during childbirth. In February 2020 the World Health Organization reported that more than 200 million women and girls alive at the time had been victims of FGM. Most often, it is practiced when the girls are under age fifteen and without their consent.

Istar, now twenty-eight, underwent the process against her will when she was six years old. She told Daughters of Eve, a women's human rights organization, about her experience. Istar had been playing outside with her younger sister and friends from the village. Though her parents were not present, there were many relatives and family friends who were. Food and sweets were served to the attendees. First, her younger sister was called into the house for the procedure. She recalls that her nightmare began when she heard the screams of her sister. "I can hear my little sister scream, I never heard such scream."[11]

Next, it was Istar's turn. Her aunt called her in. She ran away from the adults who pursued and eventually caught her, forcing her into the house. Her neighbor and two men, whom Istar describes as "children butchers,"[12] held her down and performed the procedure. The party's attendees congratulated her when it was over and gave her sweets and money, telling her that she was a special girl now.

Istar says that she has mental scars from the experience and as a mother would never victimize her own daughter in the same way. She writes, "I've blocked it out for many years pretended that it never happened but I could no longer ignore it especially after my beautiful little girl was born, I knew as a mother I couldn't let that happen to my daughter."[13] Istar and other opponents of FGM argue that it violates a girl's or woman's most basic human rights.

Raising Awareness

At times, political or sociocultural expediency is valued more than the protection of human rights. Violators of human rights can be at the government, cultural, and/or familial levels. Torture, arbitrary detention, child marriages, honor killings, and FGM are all examples of human rights violations. People who support these practices have their reasons and fervently defend them. When this happens, human rights advocates use their voices to raise awareness and make a difference for those who cannot speak. They take a step beyond simply noticing the injustice and claiming it as such. They expose the human rights violations and try to stop them. In a metaphor pertaining to activism, human rights advocate Peter Benenson famously claimed, "It is better to light a candle than curse the darkness."[14]

CHAPTER TWO

The Activists

Malala Yousafzai, one of the most well-known human rights activists in the world, began publicly advocating for girls' education in 2008. She was eleven years old and living with her family in Pakistan's Swat Valley. During this time, Afghanistan and parts of Pakistan (including the Swat Valley) were ruled by the Taliban. Under their rule, formal education for girls was banned. Yousafzai's all-girls school, along with many others, was forced to close. When her school reopened, Yousafzai attended classes and continued to advocate for the education of girls. In October 2012, when she was fourteen years old, a masked gunman boarded the bus that was taking Yousafzai home from school and asked, "Who is Malala?"[15] Then he shot her in the left side of the head. The BBC reported that a Pakistani Taliban spokesman said that his organization was responsible for carrying out the attack. After multiple surgeries and months of rehabilitation, Yousafzai recovered.

Yousafzai's journey as an activist did not end with the bullet in her head. In December 2014 she became the youngest person to win the Nobel Peace Prize. In 2020 Yousafzai graduated from Oxford University in England. She continues her global advocacy for the education of girls with Malala Fund, which according to its website, fights for all girls to receive "12 years of free, safe, quality education."[16] According to Malala Fund, there are more than 130 million girls in the world who do not attend school. Yousafzai says, "I tell my

> "I tell my story not because it is unique, but because it is the story of many girls."[17]
>
> —Malala Yousafzai, human rights activist

story not because it is unique, but because it is the story of many girls."[17]

Many children in areas of Pakistan and Afghanistan continue to struggle to get an education. After three decades of sustained conflict in Afghanistan, the United Nations International Children's Emergency Fund (UNICEF)—the UN agency responsible for protecting children's rights—estimates that there are 3.7 million children there who are not enrolled in school. In addition to war, poverty, traditional beliefs, and child marriages, Afghan children's access to educa-

Pakistani human rights activist Malala Yousafzai survived an attack by Taliban gunmen in 2009. Malala was awarded the Nobel Peace Prize in 2014, and is the youngest person ever to win the honor.

tion has been further reduced by the global COVID-19 pandemic. Because of the pandemic, many children around the world have experienced difficulty accessing education and books.

Stand-Out Young Human Rights Activists

During the pandemic, Mohib Faizy, a nineteen-year-old information technology (IT) student at the American University of Afghanistan, has used his computer skills to bring learning resources to children in Afghanistan. Faizy is the IT manager for LEARN, a nonprofit organization that focuses on education and human rights for people in conflict zones. Faizy records himself reading Pashto- and Dari-language books with positive messages for children. (Pashto and Dari are common languages in Afghanistan.) He then posts the recordings to LEARN's Facebook page. In January 2021 LEARN graduated nine students from its first digital literacy content development program. Faizy explained LEARN's future objectives for educating children to Amnesty International: "Our plan is to eventually distribute tablets preloaded with these books to help needy students who have shown their eagerness to learn and get an education. I always wanted to improve my society, so [it] is a great chance for me to serve my people."[18]

Bana Alabed is another young activist who is trying to help her people. Alabed, born in 2009, is a Syrian refugee who is raising awareness of the human suffering during Syria's civil war. When Alabed was seven years old, she provided daily accounts on Twitter of what was happening during the siege of Aleppo. During the siege, Alabed, together with her parents and two younger brothers, struggled to survive. Her tweets represented the hardships of many children caught in the crossfire of the ongoing civil war. During one of the many days of bombings, Alabed tweeted, "This is our bombed garden. I use to play on it, now nowhere to play."[19] About a week later, Alabed tweeted, "I just want to live without fear."[20] Alabed and her family experienced food and water shortages and eventually lost their house in one of the air strikes. A friend of Alabed's lost her father and brother in the

At the age of seven, Bana Alabed (shown here with her mother), used Twitter to provide daily updates on her living conditions in the city of Aleppo during the Syrian civil war.

raids. In December 2016 the Alabed family was able to evacuate Syria and settle in Turkey. Though they were living in a more stable environment after they evacuated Aleppo, Alabed's desire to help people in Syria was not extinguished.

In October 2017 Simon & Schuster published *Dear World*, Alabed's book for children detailing what the Syrian war is like from her perspective. With over 291,000 followers on Twitter, Alabed continues to raise awareness internationally on the human rights crisis in Syria. Recently, she lamented the lack of change in circumstances for children in Syria. On January 30, 2021, Alabed tweeted, "Ten years ago, the situation is as it is now, with an increase in the number of camps instead of finding a solution. The children still cling to life and dream of a better tomorrow."[21]

Amnesty International

Human rights activists like Yousafzai, Faizy, and Alabed raise awareness, provide services to people, and hold governments and individuals with power accountable for preserving human rights. There are many human rights groups for which teens volunteer. Amnesty International is one of the most well known. It was founded in 1961 initially to help prisoners of conscience, people detained for beliefs counter to the opinions of those in power. Amnesty International's founder, British lawyer Peter Benenson, was outraged when he read about the jailing of two Portuguese students whose only crime was saying something critical about their government over dinner. At the time, Portugal was under the control of a dictator. The students were arrested and imprisoned for treason. Benenson subsequently wrote an article for *The Observer* newspaper objecting to the unlawful detainment of all prisoners of conscience, in which he stated, "The most rapid way of bringing relief to Prisoners of Conscience is publicity, especially publicity among their fellow citizens."[22]

Since 1961 Amnesty International activists of all ages have protested on the streets, written letters, sent faxes and emails, called police stations, and posted on social media to raise awareness on behalf of prisoners of conscience. Amnesty International advocates send a message to people with power that the world is watching. The pressure of international and domestic attention has led governments to free many prisoners of conscience.

> "The most rapid way of bringing relief to Prisoners of Conscience is publicity, especially publicity among their fellow citizens."[22]
>
> —Peter Benenson, founder of Amnesty International

On October 16, 2008, for example, Jenni Williams, a leader of the activist movement Women of Zimbabwe Arise, was arrested and detained in Zimbabwe for leading a peaceful protest demanding immediate access to food aid. Amnesty International objected to Williams's detainment and informed its members. Activists began contacting the authorities involved in the case. Williams testifies to the organization's effectiveness when she says, "The phone calls to the police during my arrest saved me from torture and rape. The police station was so swamped they stopped picking up the phone."[23]

Amnesty International has expanded its mandate toward a broader protection of human rights. Membership is now more than 10 million people in over 150 countries and territories. Its members continue to advocate for prisoners of conscience as well as for other victims of human rights violations—such as refugees, child soldiers and child brides, indigenous people, and many others. Every year, Amnesty International achieves human rights victories around the world. In 2020 the group's members advocated for and obtained education for Rohingya refugee children in Bangladesh's camps, the release from prison of Chinese human rights lawyer Wang Quanzhang, and Saudi Arabia's announcement to stop the death penalty for crimes committed by those under age eighteen.

Young activists are important to Amnesty International's human rights objectives. The organization's Release Myanmar Peaceful Students campaign was a student-led movement that called for the release of peaceful student protesters in Myanmar. The campaign included students from Amnesty International's chapters in Australia, Norway, Germany, and the Philippines. Young people involved with the campaign organized five protests in front of Myanmar embassies and posted 18 videos and 1,291 pictures on social media. All of the detained peaceful student protesters arrested from December 2015 to April 2016 were released and their charges dropped. Victor, a youth activist from Amnesty International Norway, says, "The experience of being a part of this student team, assisting student groups from several countries in campaigning and engaging with student organizations and local student politicians to defend the peaceful Myanmar students was truly informative and inspiring."[24]

Amnesty International's leadership believes in the power of young people, as demonstrated in the Release Myanmar Peaceful Students campaign, and has published an international youth strategy to include youth perspectives and participation in the or-

Greta Thunberg—Climate Change and Human Rights

Greta Thunberg's climate activism notoriety began when she was fifteen years old and won a newspaper essay competition in 2018. Later that year, she held a sign in front of the Swedish parliament building that read, "School Strike for Climate." She began skipping school on Fridays to protest climate change. Pictures of her protesting went viral on social media. By December 2018, twenty thousand students from countries including Australia, Belgium, Japan, the United Kingdom, and the United States had joined her efforts. Since then, Thunberg, now eighteen, has become a global leader in climate change advocacy.

Some environmental activists, including Thunberg, argue that climate change is a human rights issue. On December 10, 2019, Thunberg posted on her Facebook page, "The climate crisis is the biggest threat to human rights and human rights need to be at the center of the climate crisis." She was not the first activist to make the connection, but the argument is relatively new. Greenpeace, an environmental organization, explains, "Many of our human rights, such as right to life, health, food, and an adequate standard of living, are adversely affected by climate change."

Greta Thunberg, "On human rights day, we call for climate action," Facebook, December 10, 2019. www.facebook.com/gretathunbergsweden/posts/on-human-rights-day-we-call-for-climate-action-the-climate-crisis-is-the-biggest/999155733785580.

Greenpeace International, "What Does Climate Change Have to Do with Human Rights?," December 10, 2018. www.greenpeace.org.

ganization. Amnesty International promotes the idea that young people should not only advocate for their own rights but also stand up for the rights of others. Children and teens are vulnerable to trafficking and abuse during refugee journeys, atrocities during war, early marriage, exploitive labor, being deprived of education, and other human rights abuses. In Amnesty International's Youth, Power, Action!, the organization's international youth strategy, the leadership writes, "We have to maximize the involvement of young people in our work: as members, activists, decision-makers, young human rights defenders and as rights-holders."[25]

The Red Cross

Other human rights organizations are also beginning to see the value of young advocates. Depending on the nature of their work, organizations have various roles for teens to fill. The

American Red Cross relies heavily on the activism of young people to complete its work. Its mandate is to alleviate human suffering in emergencies, thereby protecting people's human right to life and safety. Volunteers and staff train people in life-saving skills like cardiopulmonary resuscitation, organize blood drives, offer support and comfort to members of the military and their families, and prepare communities for disasters such as wildfires or hurricanes.

There are many interconnected Red Cross organizations that are part of the international humanitarian movement. Their shared goal is to mitigate suffering around the world. While independent from each other hierarchically, the American Red Cross, other national Red Cross societies, and the International Committee of the Red Cross (ICRC) work together to alleviate human rights crises. When a conflict occurs in a country that has a national Red Cross, the ICRC and the national Red Cross work together to provide relief. In war-torn areas, relief efforts include helping refugees and displaced people get access to clean water, obtain

Red Cross workers carry the stretcher of a man injured during protests against the actions of Myanmar's military.

health care, and find family members. The ICRC also promotes governmental compliance with international humanitarian law. In January 2021 the organization's key operations were in countries such as Afghanistan, Bangladesh, Colombia, Democratic Republic of the Congo, Iraq, Israel, Libya, Mexico, Myanmar, South Sudan, Sudan, and Syria.

The American Red Cross and the ICRC were founded during the same time period and for similar reasons. After witnessing the atrocities of war, activists created the organizations to care for wounded soldiers and to create national societies that would help militaries provide medical assistance. Formally established in 1863 and now based on the Geneva Conventions of 1949, the ICRC employs over twenty thousand people around the world. Additionally, there are currently 192 national Red Cross societies.

The American Red Cross became one of these national Red Cross societies in 1881. When the Civil War started in the United States in 1861, Clara Barton began collecting supplies for the soldiers. But she soon realized that she would be more useful on the battlefield. She earned the nickname Angel of the Battlefield as a result of her work providing medical care, cooking, and comforting the Union soldiers. After the war, Barton went to Europe, where she learned about efforts to form the ICRC and national societies in Geneva. She returned to the United States, founded the American Red Cross, and served as its first president for more than two decades.

Each month the American Red Cross recognizes one of its effective young activists. In September 2020 the organization spotlighted Anushka Gupta. She first began working with the American Red Cross as a student when she founded and became the president of the Cypress Ranch High School Red Cross Club. She subsequently served on the Texas Gulf Coast Region Youth Service Council and was the 2018–2019 field ambassador for the region. She interned with the Southwest and Rocky Mountains SharePoint team, a website development group. There she helped program a website that tracks the locations of emergency response vehicles and the supplies on them. For their work on the website, the team won the Red Cross Presidential Award for Excellence.

Human Rights Watch

Human Rights Watch (HRW) is another organization that promotes human rights around the world. HRW (originally known as Helsinki Watch) was created in 1978 in connection with the Helsinki Accords, a nonbinding pledge of thirty-five nations to respect human rights. HRW's purpose is to hold those countries accountable to their pledge. Its workforce—which includes lawyers, journalists, and academics in over one hundred countries—investigates and exposes human rights violations and works to change policy to protect vulnerable people. HRW experts focus on many humanitarian crises, currently including Syria's civil war, mass killings in the Philippines, and persecution of the Rohingya ethnic group in Myanmar.

HRW monitors and provides information on the circumstances of vulnerable populations and pushes decision makers for change. In cases of systemic human rights violations, the organization advocates for international pressure on offending states, justice in which perpetrators are brought to trial, and changes in laws that violate human rights. HRW acknowledges the importance of partnerships. The organization writes, "Change doesn't come easily, and in some cases it can be painfully slow. And it rarely comes from our efforts alone, but rather from the combined efforts of numerous groups and activists."[26]

HRW's permanent staff sometimes works in partnerships with young human rights activists. For example, HRW's Children's Rights Division works with youth activists and others to reduce the incarceration of children under age eighteen. The group's partnerships with young people and other advocates in California, for instance, have resulted in many legal changes that decrease the likelihood that young people will be prosecuted criminally as adults.

Little Miss Flint Continues Her Activism

Mari Copeny, a thirteen-year-old from Flint, Michigan, who refers to herself as Little Miss Flint, became an activist when she was only eight years old. In April 2014 Flint changed its water source to the Flint River, which was corrosive and carried lead from the pipes to the people's water supply. Twelve people died and more than eighty others became sick from the contaminated water. Copeny witnessed the effects of the polluted water firsthand. She was worried especially about her younger sister, who developed terrible rashes on her skin. Copeny wrote a letter to then-president Barack Obama describing Flint's water situation and asking for a chance to meet the president and first lady. As a result, Obama visited the city and subsequently provided $100 million in federal aid to address the water problem.

Emboldened by the realization that young people can bring about change, Copeny continues her activism for Flint's children. She says, "So many kids here in Flint go without." In the Flint Kids Read campaign, she has organized the donation of thousands of books and seventeen thousand backpacks equipped with school supplies. She also organized a Christmas 2020 toy donation for Flint's children.

Quoted in Ellen Chamberlain, "Little Miss Flint Wants to Give Back to the Children of Flint—and You Can Help," The Gander, December 17, 2020. https://gandernewsroom.com.

HRW further offers templates of letters that address various human rights issues. The templates are available to young activists and others who want to contact lawmakers or other important decision makers. For example, young activists can send a template letter to automobile companies doing business in Saudi Arabia. The template letter encourages them to pressure the government to release the women from prison who advocated for women's right to drive cars. For example, in December 2020 Saudi women's rights activist Loujain al-Hathloul was sentenced to five years and eight months in prison in a court usually used for terrorism and national security cases. Because Saudi Arabia lifted its ban on women's ability to drive in June 2018, HRW reasons that car companies are making more money now because of activists like Hathloul and the increase of potential drivers in Saudi Arabia. Moreover, HRW is encour-

> "The arc of the universe may bend toward justice, but it doesn't bend on its own."[27]
>
> —Barack Obama, former US president

aging human rights advocates to send the online template letter to persuade car manufacturers to put pressure on the Saudi government to release the women who helped them increase their profits.

Young Activists Are Essential

There are many young exemplary figures in the fight for human rights. Young advocates work together inside or in partnership with human rights organizations to affect change. The work they do is essential, as President Barack Obama noted in a 2013 speech commemorating the life and work of Martin Luther King Jr. "The arc of the universe may bend toward justice," Obama said, "but it doesn't bend on its own."[27]

CHAPTER THREE

The Teen Activist's Tool Kit

Social media is one of the most important tools for teen activists. Rahaf Mohammed might have saved her own life with her use of Twitter. In January 2019 Mohammed, who was eighteen years old at the time, fled from her traditional Saudi family during their vacation to Kuwait. She alleges that her family members physically abused her for perceived offenses such as refusing to marry and cutting her hair. Seizing the opportunity to travel internationally without having permission from a male relative in Kuwait, Mohammed boarded a flight to Australia with a layover in Thailand. There, a Saudi official confiscated her passport, leaving her trapped in Thailand under the imminent threat of deportation. Mohammed feared for her life, because she not only refused to follow social norms in Saudi Arabia and had run away from her family but had also renounced Islam—a crime punishable by death. She barricaded her airport hotel room door, where she stayed for six days, and took her case to Twitter. She writes, "I'm afraid my family WILL kill me. . . . They will kill me because I fled and because I announced my atheism. They wanted me to pray and to wear a veil, and I didn't want to."[28]

All over the world, human rights activists, including from organizations like HRW, saw Mohammed's pleas on Twitter and advocated for her. *The Guardian* reports that other media outlets were slower to pick up the story, but social

> "I'm afraid my family WILL kill me. . . . They will kill me because I fled and because I announced my atheism."[28]
>
> —Rahaf Mohammed, an eighteen-year-old activist

media brought her case to the surface immediately. #SaveRahaf became the social media battle cry for human rights defenders at that time. Canada was the first to offer Mohammed sanctuary as a refugee, six days after her journey began. In comparison, the process for applying for refugee status in the United States usually takes an average of two years. A week after her flight to Thailand, 176,000 people were following Mohammed on Twitter. Her savvy use of social media prompted this comment from a Saudi official: "I wish you had taken her phone, it would have been better than (taking) her passport."[29] Two years later, in January 2021—with over 229,000 Twitter followers—Mohammed's activism for the rights of women and refugees continued.

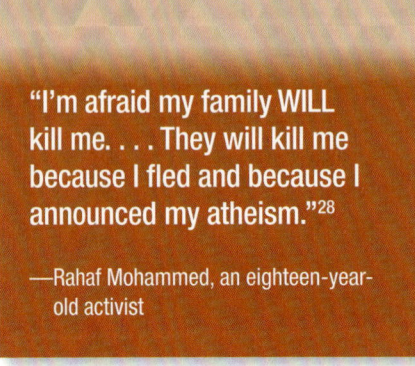

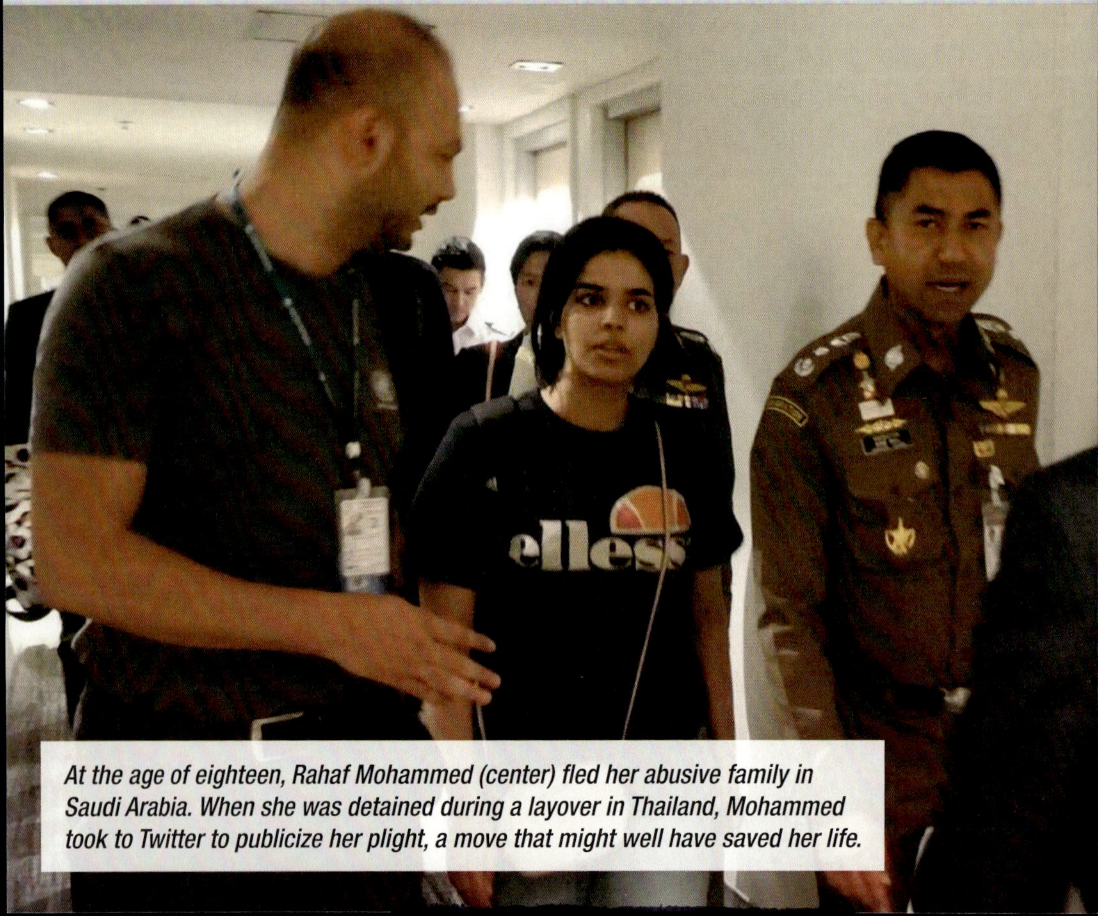

At the age of eighteen, Rahaf Mohammed (center) fled her abusive family in Saudi Arabia. When she was detained during a layover in Thailand, Mohammed took to Twitter to publicize her plight, a move that might well have saved her life.

Using Social Media to Fight for Human Rights

Social media users who took an interest in Mohammed's plight and helped spread her story were advocating for her human rights. Social media can raise awareness more quickly and among more people than other media outlets. Whether posted on the internet or reported by a news outlet, there is no shortage of tragic stories of human rights violations. But the framing of a story with the most effective hashtag on social media can make all the difference in raising it to prominence.

Behrouz Boochani, a Kurdish refugee from Iran, launched an effective social media campaign, but the outcomes were slower than in Mohammed's case. After seven years in detention, Boochani was granted refugee status in New Zealand in July 2020. As a journalist from an ethnic minority who was under scrutiny and feared persecution in his home country, Boochani, then thirty, fled Iran in 2013. He flew to Indonesia and paid to be smuggled to Australia on a small boat across the Indian Ocean. The first boat he took sank. The passengers were saved by a fisher and taken back to Indonesia. Boochani knew he would likely die or go to prison if he returned to Iran. He decided to continue to Australia despite the dangerous journey. During his second attempt, the boat was overcrowded but successfully made the voyage to Australian waters. That same week, however, Australian prime minister Kevin Rudd announced that migrants arriving by boat without a visa would not be settled in Australia. They were instead transferred to a detainment facility on Manus Island in Papua New Guinea.

While detained, Boochani secretly used a smuggled phone to take videos of the detainees' treatment in the facility. He posted the footage to Twitter; it showed cramped living quarters and illustrated the distress and depression that refugees felt about an uncertain future. Boochani also maintained a Facebook account, followed by thousands of journalists, to which he posted detailed written descriptions of his life in detainment. His social media profile gave him notoriety to draw even more attention to his own situation, as well as to the daily life of detainees on Manus Island.

Some of the hunger strikes and riots there had already made news headlines, but Boochani wanted to expose the psychological effects of indefinite detainment and anonymity on the facility's detainees. In *The Guardian* he writes, "It is a type of profound and annihilating torture. Living constantly under the petrifying sledge hammer, having a destroyed past and imagining a dark future give a person a sense of being crushed."[30] In addition to writing a book and news articles—and making proficient use of social media—Boochani sent his phone recordings over WhatsApp to Holland-based Iranian filmmaker Arash Kamali Sarvestani. With the footage, Sarvestani produced the documentary film *Chauka, Please Tell Us the Time*. Just as Mohammed was able to use social media to attract global attention to a personal human rights concern, Boochani's use of social media led to broader sustained attention to the plight of asylum seekers at Australia's immigration detention centers.

Social Media for Group Organizing

Social media's ability to bring attention and sympathy to an individual case and/or human rights abuses is evidenced by Boochani, Mohammed, and many others. Polling by the Pew Research Center in July 2020 found that overall, eight out of ten Americans say that social media platforms are either very or somewhat effective in raising public awareness for social and political issues. In addition to raising awareness, social media also is used to organize groups for an event or around a cause. Facebook in particular has been widely used to notify potentially interested members of online as well as in-person opportunities for advocacy.

Human rights activists have used social media platforms to protest the prolonged detainment and family separations of asylum seekers occurring at the US border. Lights for Liberty—which has the stated goal of ending human concentration camps—used social media to plan seven hundred events and protests in all US states on July 12, 2019. The protests pertained to the

Human rights activists have made effective use of social media to organize protests, such as this one decrying American immigration policies of separating refugee children from their parents.

treatment of asylum seekers in the United States. The events gained significant media attention, including headlines in newspapers such as the *Washington Post* and *USA Today*.

The Importance of Listening

In addition to their social media navigation abilities, teen advocates for human rights can be assets to their causes if they have good communication skills. Listening is at the heart of effective communication. Teen activists must open their hearts to the stories of others and consider different perspectives and the multitude of people involved. In short, they must be willing to listen and learn. Suzanne Degges-White, a licensed counselor and professor, emphasizes the importance of listening for advocacy. In *Psychology Today*, she writes, "When building an alliance with

> "When building an alliance with those for whom you would like to advocate, get their story before trying to fight their fight."[31]
>
> —Suzanne Degges-White, licensed counselor and professor

Listening is always important, but perhaps even more so for issues in human rights advocacy. In many circumstances, advocates come from different cultures and life situations than those for whom they advocate. In the case of child marriages and FGM for example, there are many human rights activists within the cultures who oppose these traditions, but a large number of people who advocate against these practices are cultural outsiders. It is imperative to consider the culture and not to alienate families.

Casting parents as villains in the fight for children's human rights is not productive, because there is much more to the story. Parents love their children and are usually trying to do what they think is best for them. In some circumstances though, like when there are limited economic and educational opportunities, parents feel they have few options for their children. For example, child marriage is common in Niger partly because it is the norm but also because poor families often struggle to provide basic necessities for their children. Many families arrange their daughters' marriages when they are under eighteen years old as a way to provide for them when the family cannot. With the daughter out of the house, there are also more resources for the other children living there. In addition to limited food in some houses, education is also a precious commodity. Education in primary and secondary schools in Niger is low. UNICEF reports that only 80 percent of students in Niger finish primary school and less than half finish secondary school. UNICEF further finds that the adult literacy rate in Niger is low—42 percent of the men and 14 percent of the women are literate. There is not much economic opportunity for the illiterate. In order to address the high rates of child marriage in Niger, human rights advocates need to consider

Cartoons Stir Emotions

Cartoons are a form of creative expression that tend to induce a multitude of emotional reactions. On October 17, 2020, a middle school history teacher named Samuel Paty was killed with multiple stab wounds to the neck in a suburb of Paris, France. Earlier that month, in a lesson about free expression, he had shown his students cartoons of the Prophet Muhammad, which is considered blasphemous by Muslims. Witnesses to the teacher's murder reportedly heard the eighteen-year-old unnamed attacker shout, "Allahu Akbar," or "God is greatest."

While the murder in the Parisian suburb represents the darkest reaction and a threat to free expression, human rights activists sometimes use cartoons to elicit sympathy and understanding. In 2018, on the seventieth anniversary of the Universal Declaration of Human Rights (UDHR), the Cartoon Movement, the Office of the United Nations High Commissioner for Human Rights, and the government of the Netherlands launched a cartoon competition to emphasize the importance of the document. A committee selected thirty winning cartoons—one for each article of the UDHR—of the five hundred cartoons submitted from around the world. The cartoons are helpful to illustrate what human rights are. Teen activists can use their artistic skills to spread the message about the meaning and importance of human rights.

---

access to food and education, as well as economic opportunities, for the people there.

In many of the cases where girls are married very young, they tend to blame circumstances but not their own parents. Hadiza, for example, who was married at age fourteen in Niger because her father's youngest brother could not pay a debt, recognizes her mother's grief when Hadiza was married. She says, "My mum cried for two weeks straight. She even had problems with her eyes as a result."[32] Advocating against child marriages means listening to marginalized voices and speaking out against the practice. It also means helping them fight the system that led to a widespread violation of their basic rights—such as food shortages and lack of access to education and economic opportunities—rather than simply villainizing their parents. Being a human rights advocate means listening intently and considering all the angles.

Writing for Human Rights

After listening and learning, writing is an effective method with which to advocate for human rights. Peter Benenson founded Amnesty International to advocate for prisoners of conscience. Other human rights organizations have followed suit. These campaigns have included writing on behalf of people who have been deprived of their freedom because of their opinions. As letters pour in and inundate decision makers, human rights advocates believe the mounting pressure ignites the flame of justice and leads to many of the prisoners being released. There are many opportunities to support human rights with writing, such as in Amnesty International's Write for Rights campaign.

Human rights advocates around the world are writing letters on behalf of Germain Rukuki, for example, who is detained in the Republic of Burundi, a landlocked country in East Africa. Rukuki is currently being held on a thirty-two-year sentence in Ngozi Prison, where he and 120 other inmates share a cell that has two showers and two toilets. Rukuki, a human rights defender, was arrested on July 13, 2017, in the middle of the night. In April 2018 he was found guilty of rebellion and other related charges. Rukuki had worked for Action by Christians for Abolition of Torture (ACAT-Burundi), an antitorture organization that opposed President Pierre Nkurunziza in his bid for a third term. By the time of Rukuki's arrest, the government had already shut down ACAT-Burundi, but the charges were related to his prior activity with the organization. Rukuki has not been permitted visitation from his family, including his youngest son, who was born after his arrest. Ironically, Rukuki lost his freedom for speaking up for people who had no voice. Human rights defenders write on his behalf for justice and to return the favor.

There are many opportunities for teens to use their writing skills to support human rights. Aside from form letters at large human rights organizations, advocates can research the legislation being considered at the local, state, and national levels in their own countries. If legislation under consideration is a threat to human rights, teen activists can write their own personal letter or email to relevant decision makers. Creating a form letter and getting other teens involved in a writing campaign is another potentially effective strategy to amplify a perspective.

Speaking for Human Rights

An activist can also literally amplify a perspective with a megaphone. Teens appear in newspaper images around the world speaking their messages, sometimes into megaphones, at protests. On June 4, 2020, six teens who met on Twitter and call themselves Teens 4 Equality organized a protest against racial injustice. The protest drew a crowd of about ten thousand people in Nashville, Tennessee. The teen organizers—Nya Collins, Jade Fuller, Kennedy Green, Emma Rose Smith, Mikayla Smith, and Zee Thomas—sought an end to police brutality. On June 8, 2020, following the protest, Nashville mayor John Cooper announced that the city's police department would more broadly use body cameras to monitor police encounters beginning the following month.

Organized protests such as this Black Lives Matter march held in in Nashville, Tennessee, in 2020 are an effective way for activists to deliver their message to local officials.

Teen human rights activists have also spoken in front of policy makers to plead their cases. In May 2019, EJ Carroll and Katrina Lambert, both eighteen years old at the time, addressed the UN's Committee Against Torture about Scotland's human rights record. They spoke about incorporating more rights for children into Scottish domestic law—such as the age of criminal responsibility and the practice of restraining young children in schools. According to *The National*, a Scottish newspaper, Carroll and Lambert believe that it should be the norm for decision makers to listen to young people, not the exception. Lambert says, "Young people have such a powerful voice and when they are given a platform that is shown. Adults often underestimate the power they can have."[33]

> "Young people have such a powerful voice and when they are given a platform that is shown. Adults often underestimate the power they can have."[33]
>
> —Katrina Lambert, an eighteen-year-old who spoke in front the UN's Committee Against Torture

Changing Hearts and Minds

Teens can make a difference, and communication is paramount to the process of change. Sometimes even little ripples can make big waves. Organization and planning are important, but not all opportunities are on stages in front of the United Nations or leading thousands in protest. There are many ways to make a difference locally.

Teens can, for example, engage in thoughtful conversations with people who might disagree with their perspectives. In day-to-day discussions, anecdotes of real people tend to sway opinions more than statistics. For example, in the United States, there is political polarization on immigration and refugee policy. When an advocate discusses the plight of a real person who escaped persecution in his or her home country, made a harrowing journey on a dinghy across the ocean, and needs sanctuary, the listener is more likely to feel empathy than if he or she is flooded with statistics. Volunteering at a soup kitchen can also make an important

Mai Khoi Sings for Human Rights

Some activists leverage their vocal talents to support human rights. Mai Khoi, sometimes referred to as the Lady Gaga of Vietnam, left Vietnam in November 2019 after claiming that police threatened her for demanding the release of a dissident friend. In 2021 Khoi was living in Pittsburgh, Pennsylvania, where she studies English and continues to work on her music. Many of her songs express messages of dissent, such as opposition to censorship and Vietnam's one-party political system. For her work, in 2018 the Human Rights Foundation awarded Khoi the Václav Havel Prize for Creative Dissent.

Khoi rose to fame for her patriotic song "Vietnam" in 2010 but began to fall out of favor with the state when she started publicly advocating for women's and LGBTQ rights. In 2016 she nominated herself for a seat in the National Assembly of Vietnam. Her name was removed from the ballot, however, and her concerts subjected to police raids. Known for culturally atypical things like having dyed hair and refusing to wear a bra, Khoi was outraged when a government censor showed up to her rehearsal to object to her wardrobe. She says, "They wanted famous people like me to be the right model for everyone in the country, of the traditional Vietnamese woman."

Quoted in Scott Mervis, "Mai Khoi, 'the Lady Gaga of Vietnam,' Finds a Safe Space in Pittsburgh to Create 'Bad Activist,'" *Pittsburgh (PA) Post-Gazette*, January 27, 2021. www.post-gazette.com.

---

difference in someone's day. Being kind to a refugee at school and including the person in social activities might change his or her life. These are some of the small actions that lead to the big victories in human rights advocacy.

There are many useful skills for being an activist. While big events like public protests and walkouts are important, a significant role for young human rights activists is to keep their eyes open for opportunities to be advocates locally at their schools or around their dinner tables. They should also keep their hearts open to stories different from their own, consider contextual factors, and listen to how they might be able to help marginalized voices. Being a human rights activist does not mean having all the answers. Rather, advocating for human rights means carefully considering the important questions and finding where one might fit in the pursuit of a solution.

CHAPTER FOUR

Risks and Rights

Internationally, human rights activists are in grave danger at times. Malala Yousafzai's story is a sobering reminder of the potential risks that people take when they advocate for human rights. Yousafzai's risks were extraordinary because she had few formal rights as a human rights advocate in the Swat Valley of Pakistan at the time she was shot. The rule of law there was unstable. Additionally, people who implemented what they perceived as justice were violent and not held accountable. In contrast, activists in the United States face some risks, but there are institutions in place intended to protect them.

Rights in the United States

In the United States the Constitution guarantees free speech and the right of assembly. The Bill of Rights, the first ten amendments to the Constitution, safeguards individual liberties from the powers of government. For example, the Eighth Amendment forbids cruel or unusual punishment. Therefore, if a person is accused of a crime and arrested in the United States, there is a process by which law enforcement officers and legal system personnel have to deal with that individual. Unlike in Syria and many other places, police officers in the United States cannot accuse a person of a crime and then engage in torture to obtain a confession. The Eighth Amendment is meant to offer the accused person protection from being treated unfairly.

Perhaps most significant for human rights advocates in the United States is the First Amendment, which protects freedom of speech, the press, and religion and the right to peacefully protest. Whereas there are many regimes in countries around the world imprisoning people simply for having opinions that oppose the government, would-be prisoners of conscience in the United States are protected by the First Amendment.

The Bill of Rights governs students in primary and secondary public schools as well as adults in the United States. The freedom of speech and the press, more specifically, applies to teens in public schools but is more limited in private schools. According to the American Civil Liberties Union (ACLU), an organization that defends constitutional rights and liberties, "[Students] have the right to speak out, hand out flyers and petitions, and wear expressive clothing in school—as long as [they] don't disrupt the functioning of the school or violate the school's content-neutral policies."[34] For example, students have the right to wear a shirt with a message supporting a human right or a human rights organization as long as it does not contain expletives or disruptive content or is not otherwise in violation of the school's clothing policies. In brief, while the school is able to ban swear words, it cannot ban the expression of political opinions.

> "[Students] have the right to speak out, hand out flyers and petitions, and wear expressive clothing in school—as long as [they] don't disrupt the functioning of the school or violate the school's content-neutral policies."[34]
>
> —American Civil Liberties Union

Student Rights in Private Schools

The constitutional rights of students in private schools in the United States are less expansive. In public schools, for example, free speech extends to social media. According to the ACLU, public schools cannot penalize students for their messages posted "off campus and outside of school hours that does not relate

43

to school."[35] Because private schools are not extensions of the government and there are different codes of conduct to which parents and students agree to adhere, students' rights are less clear in private schools.

In January 2020 Louisville, Kentucky's, Whitefield Academy, a private Christian school, expelled a student after she posted a picture on social media. In the picture, the student was celebrating her fifteenth birthday (outside of school) wearing a rainbow sweater, with a rainbow cake placed in front of her at the table. The student's mother, Kimberly Alford, tells the *Louisville Courier*

Protesters march in favor of LGBTQ rights. Public schools are not allowed to prevent students from expressing political opinions as long as their activities do not interfere with normal school functions.

Journal that Whitefield Academy's head of school, Bruce Jacobson, sent her an email notifying Alford of her daughter's immediate expulsion due to her post on social media. According to Alford, Jacobson claims that the picture "demonstrates a posture of morality and cultural acceptance contrary to that of Whitefield Academy's beliefs."[36] The private school's student handbook states, "The atmosphere or conduct within a particular home may be counter . . . to the biblical lifestyle the school teaches. This includes . . . sexual immorality [or] homosexual orientation . . . In such cases, the school reserves the right, within its sole discretion, to . . . discontinue enrollment of a student."[37] In the end, the fifteen-year-old student was expelled for her out-of-school picture on social media of rainbows, assumed to symbolize her support of LGBTQ rights, which is an expression that explicitly violates the school handbook. Following the expulsion, the student enrolled in a public school.

Other Risks on Social Media

While the social media incident at Whitefield Academy would have concluded differently in a public school, advocating for human rights on social media could have other consequences. Even in public schools, if messages are posted with school computers or during school hours, students might be subject to penalties. These penalties vary by states and localities, but some cases regarding students' rights to free expression in schools have made their way to the US Supreme Court.

In January 2021, for example, the Supreme Court announced that it would hear a case involving a First Amendment challenge to Mahanoy Area High School's cheerleading rules. In 2017 a fifteen-year-old cheerleader referred to as B.L. posted a picture on Snapchat outside of school hours and off school property in which she and her friend posed in front of a convenience store holding up their middle fingers, with the superimposed text "f*** school f*** softball f*** cheer f*** everything."[38] Pennsylvania's

Chechen Teen Human Rights Activist Tortured on Video

On September 5, 2020, Chechen security forces kidnapped Salman Tepsurkayev, age nineteen, from his hotel room and detained him at a nearby police compound, according to HRW. Previously, Tepsurkayev had worked as a moderator for a social media news channel known for criticizing Chechnya's leader, Ramzan Kadyrov. Kadyrov has been accused of human rights abuses, including torture and disappearances. Two days after his arrest, Tepsurkayev appeared naked in a video posted on social media. In it, he says, "I am punishing myself." He then apologizes and sits down on a glass bottle. In a video posted to a progovernment Instagram channel two days later, Tepsurkayev claims that he made the video because he regretted things he said about the government.

The Chechen government office of human rights has said that the video is unacceptable but declined to investigate because Tepsurkayev has not filed a complaint. In January 2021 Russian state investigators opened a criminal case concerning the kidnapping of Tepsurkayev. As of February 2021, he remained missing.

Quoted in "Chechen Teen Who Appeared in Humiliation Video Was Kidnapped, Russian Paper Says," Radio Free Europe/Radio Liberty, September 9, 2020. www.rferl.org.

Mahanoy Area High School officials were notified. After deeming the post to be "negative, disrespectful and demeaning,"[39] they barred B.L. from participating on the junior varsity cheerleading team. The ACLU of Pennsylvania, arguing on behalf of B.L. that the school was violating her First Amendment rights, took her case to court. In June 2020 a federal appeals court ruled in favor of B.L. and the ACLU of Pennsylvania that "public schools cannot censor students' off-campus speech based on a fear of disruption of school activities."[40] The Supreme Court, which has final say in US federal law, was slated to hear oral arguments regarding this case in the spring of 2021.

If a teen human rights advocate decides to post a social media message with lewd or disruptive content, he or she should be aware that there might be risks involved. Even when human rights advocacy on social media is protected by the First Amendment, teen activists might still experience social stigma or alienation from peers who disagree with their views.

School Walkouts

In addition to other penalties, student activists might experience social stigma when they participate in other forms of human rights advocacy, such as walkouts. A walkout is a departure from work or school, sometimes planned and other times spontaneous. Students in schools across the United States have planned walkouts pertaining to issues such as racial justice, LGBTQ rights, gun violence in schools, sexual assault, bullying, and other causes. According to the ACLU, public schools can punish students for walkouts because they are missing class, but not more harshly for the political content of the reason they miss class. The ACLU encourages students who plan to participate in a walkout to review their school's policies for missing class. Talking with teachers or administrators beforehand might also be a productive avenue with which to affect change. Sometimes people with positions of authority at the school will work with the students, but other times they might not.

One month after the mass shooting at Marjory Stoneman Douglas High School in Parkland, Florida, students around the nation staged a walkout. The intent of the March 14, 2018, walkout was to encourage US lawmakers to pass stricter gun control legislation. Women's March Youth Empower, the organizer of the walkout, encouraged students to leave their classes at 10:00 a.m. for seventeen minutes, to represent the seventeen lives lost in the Parkland shooting. Prior to the national walkout, the National Association of Secondary School Principals advised teachers and staff against participating. The professional organization for middle school and high school principals writes, "Students with differing views might feel alienated or compelled to participate in a protest against their will if school officials are perceived as supporting the protest."[41] The decision of whether or

> "Students with differing views might feel alienated or compelled to participate in a protest against their will if school officials are perceived as supporting the protest."[41]
>
> —National Association of Secondary School Principals

One month after the 2018 mass shooting at Marjory Stoneman Douglas High School in Parkland, Florida, students around the nation, including from this school in Tucson, Arizona, staged walkouts.

not to participate in the walkouts likely led to instances of social stigmatization for some students. Additionally, in Allentown, Pennsylvania, more than two hundred students were given a Saturday detention for their decision to participate in the walkout. Punishments varied across school districts throughout the United States.

Almost two years after the national walkout, in February 2020, students at Kennedy Catholic High School staged a mass walkout to protest the firing of two teachers. On Valentine's Day 2020, the private school in the suburbs of Seattle, Washington, announced the termination of its English teacher, Paul Danforth, and soccer coach, Michelle Beattie. Both employees were involved in same-sex relationships and had recently become engaged to their partners. During one of the many protests that month, students held signs in the schoolyard in support of LGBTQ rights and hoisted a rainbow pride flag up the school's flagpole. While the walkout and protests did not get Danforth and Beattie their jobs back, they did bring national attention to the employment termination of two people because of their sexual orientation.

Social alienation, detention, and suspension were possible consequences of the national walkout and the localized walkout at Kennedy Catholic. It is unclear whether Kennedy Catholic punished the students for missing class, but the school would have been within its rights if it had, according to school rules. Prior to the protest, a senior at Kennedy Catholic, Jacqueline Southwell, told CBS News that she was not aware of any student at the school who was not participating in the walkout. In the end, hundreds of the school's students participated. In the event that friend groups were split over whether to participate in walkouts over gun violence in 2018 or at Kennedy Catholic in 2020, it is likely that some students were alienated for their action or inaction.

Peaceful Protests

In addition to events that have promoted LGBTQ rights, there have been many peaceful protests across the United States that support other human rights as well. For example, teens across the country have been participating in large numbers in protests for racial equality and against police killings of unarmed Black men and women. The First Amendment in the Bill of Rights guarantees people the right to assemble peacefully and to state their disagreements and problems with the government. Even still, there are risks associated with peaceful protests. Sometimes activists get arrested, and other times, violence occurs and injuries result.

The police killing of George Floyd, a Black American, echoed across the nation on May 25, 2020. Protests began nationwide after a video of the incident leading to his death went viral. Activists contend that police officer Derek Chauvin's actions and the complacency of the officers with him constitute police brutality. Many of them say that the officers would have treated Floyd differently in the same circumstances if he were White.

While most of the protests have been peaceful, some have not—leading to destruction of businesses and attacks on police officers. On July 17, 2020, for example, there was a coordinated attack on police officers in Grant Park in Chicago, Illinois. As

Teen Activist Faces Imprisonment in Hong Kong

In December 2020 Tony Chung, age nineteen, was sentenced to four months in prison for taking part in a protest and insulting China's flag. During a demonstration in May 2019, Chung threw China's flag to the ground during a confrontation with a pro-China group. Chung further founded the now disbanded group supporting Hong Kong's independence called Studentlocalism. He is a prodemocracy activist in Hong Kong, which is a semiautonomous region of China. Hong Kong's court has further charged Chung with inciting secession, a crime that carries a maximum sentence of life imprisonment. In January 2021 his case was moved to the District Court, where maximum sentences are capped at seven years.

Chung is the second person to be charged under China's new national security law, passed in May 2020. Despite an agreement that Hong Kong would maintain judicial independence, China imposed the security law on the territory to simplify the prosecution of peaceful protesters. Joshua Rosenzweig, the head of Amnesty International's China team, said that Chung's arrest was "politically motivated" and "expose[s] the Hong Kong government's disdain for freedom of expression and dissent."

Quoted in Britt Clennett, "Hong Kong Teen Activist Charged Under Security Law After Being Detained Near US Consulate," ABC News, October 29, 2020. https://abcnews.go.com.

thousands took part in protesting peacefully, the city's overhead video surveillance showed at least a dozen people holding black umbrellas to shield a group of people underneath. The group under the umbrellas made their way to police officers posted at a Christopher Columbus statue. There, attackers in all black threw frozen water bottles, rocks, and explosive devices at the officers. The *Chicago Tribune* reports that forty-nine Chicago police officers were injured, and eighteen of them needed to be treated at the hospital.

Protest Risks

Because some protests turn violent, tensions are high at times on both sides of the line—for the protesters and the law enforcement officials trying to maintain order. There are risks associated with participating in protests. Many protesters opposing police brutality triggered by the killing of George Floyd have been pepper sprayed and shot with rubber bullets. In Seattle a seven-year-old boy holding his father's hand was pepper sprayed in the face by the police in June 2020. Also in June 2020, Aly Conyers, age seventeen, was hit with pepper spray near the White House in Washington, DC, while supporting justice for Floyd. Conyers, a student at a South Carolina high school, had stood on a brick platform with a megaphone hours before getting pepper sprayed. Regarding the incident, she said, "It was terrifying. It was like something out of a movie scene. Everyone went moving backwards and crying."[42]

> "It was terrifying. It was like something out of a movie scene. Everyone went moving backwards and crying."[42]
>
> —Aly Conyers, a seventeen-year-old pepper sprayed at a protest

Similarly, in Minneapolis, Chris Owusu, age seventeen, was chanting Floyd's name when he was hit with pepper spray, and his friend was shot in the forehead with a rubber bullet during a protest. Owusu explains in an interview that the pepper spray burned his eyes and made him feel as though his lungs were collapsing. He says, "It's the most excruciating pain that I've ever

This protest in Los Angeles of the police killing of George Floyd in 2020 turned violent. Protesters should be aware of the risks associated with demonstrations that become violent.

felt."[43] Activists should be aware that sometimes, even peaceful protesters experience physical injuries.

It is also worth remembering that police officers are responsible for protecting members of the public and for maintaining law and order. In fulfilling these roles, they are allowed to use a limited amount of force—but this depends on the circumstances. Further, the amount of force used must be reasonable. Young activists who believe police have used excessive force during a protest might be able to file a claim or lawsuit against the police, but proving such a claim can be difficult and costly.

Young human rights activists encounter different risks and have different rights, depending on where they are. Some have lost life and liberty, and others have been tear-gassed or shot with rubber bullets. Additionally, while the Bill of Rights protects speech and freedom of expression in the United States, some of those rights are limited for students in schools. Perhaps most importantly, even with institutional protections, circumstances at protests or other events produce unforeseen risks for human rights advocates.

SOURCE NOTES

Introduction: Young People for Human Rights
1. Quoted in Women Deliver, "Divina Stella Maloum," 2020. https://womendeliver.org.
2. Quoted in Ammeno Dayo, "14-Year-Old Cameroonian, Divina Maloum Wins International Peace Prize," African Exponent, November 21, 2019. www.africanexponent.com.
3. Quoted in Dayo, "14-Year-Old Cameroonian, Divina Maloum Wins International Peace Prize."
4. Quoted in Camille Roch, "10 Quotes on the Power of Human Rights Education," Amnesty International, February 10, 2016. www.amnesty.org.

Chapter One: The Issue Is Human Rights
5. Quoted in Anne Barnard, "Inside Syria's Secret Torture Prisons: How Bashar al-Assad Crushed Dissent," *New York Times*, May 11, 2019. www.nytimes.com.
6. Quoted in BBC, "Mohammad Hassan Rezaiee: UN Condemns Iran over 'Juvenile Execution,'" December 31, 2020. www.bbc.com.
7. Quoted in Carol Rosenberg, "Architect of C.I.A. Interrogation Program Testifies at Guantánamo Bay," *New York Times*, January 21, 2020. www.nytimes.com.
8. Quoted in Office of the United Nations High Commissioner for Human Rights, "Torture Is Torture, and Waterboarding Is Not an Exception—UN Expert Urges the US Not to Reinstate It," January 30, 2017. www.ohchr.org.
9. Quoted in *India Today*, "*Chhapaak*: Who Is Laxmi Agarwal, the Acid Attack Survivor Deepika Padukone Is Playing?," March 25, 2019. www.indiatoday.in.
10. Quoted in Lucy Anna Gray, "Forgotten Women," *The Independent* (London), March 24, 2019. www.independent.co.uk.
11. Quoted in Daughters of Eve, "Stopping FGM, Istar's Story." www.dofeve.org.
12. Quoted in Daughters of Eve, "Stopping FGM, Istar's Story."
13. Quoted in Daughters of Eve, "Stopping FGM, Istar's Story."
14. Quoted in *New York Times*, "Peter Benenson, Founder of Amnesty International," February 28, 2005. www.nytimes.com.

Chapter Two: The Activists

15. Quoted in Malala Fund, "Malala's Story," 2021. https://malala.org.
16. Malala Fund, "Our Work," 2021. https://malala.org.
17. Quoted in Malala Fund, "Malala's Story."
18. Quoted in Sara Vida Coumans, "Seven Young People Who Had Great Ideas During COVID-19," Amnesty International, July 30, 2020. www.amnesty.org.
19. Bana Alabed (@AlabedBana), "This is our bombed garden. I use to play on it, now nowhere to play," Twitter, October 4, 2016, 6:54 a.m. https://twitter.com/AlabedBana/status/783258925575593984.
20. Bana Alabed (@AlabedBana), "I just want to live without fear," Twitter, October 12, 2016, 9:54 a.m. https://twitter.com/AlabedBana/status/786204553121263616.
21. Bana Alabed (@AlabedBana), "Ten years ago, the situation is as it is now, with an increase in the number of camps instead of finding a solution," Twitter, January 30, 2021, 7:55 a.m. https://twitter.com/AlabedBana/status/1355499813886976002.
22. Peter Benenson, "The Forgotten Prisoners," *The Observer* (London), May 28, 1961, p. 1.
23. Quoted in Amnesty International, "Detention and Imprisonment." www.amnesty.org.
24. Quoted in Amnesty International, "Student-Led Campaign Calling for Release of Myanmar Peaceful Students," 2017. www.amnesty.org.
25. Amnesty International, "Youth, Power, Action! International Youth Strategy, 2017–2020," 2016. www.amnesty.org.
26. Human Rights Watch. "Impact," 2021. www.hrw.org.
27. Quoted in Zeke Miller, "In Commemorative MLK Speech, President Obama Recalls His Own 2008 Dream," *Time*, August 28, 2013. https://swampland.time.com.

Chapter Three: The Teen Activist's Tool Kit

28. Quoted in Catherine Porter, "Saudi Teenager Who Fled Family Embraces All Things Canadian," *New York Times*, January 14, 2019. www.nytimes.com.
29. Quoted in Helen Davidson, "Rahaf and Hakeem: Why Has One Refugee Captured the World's Attention While Another Is Left in Jail?," *The Guardian* (Manchester, UK), January 10, 2019. www.theguardian.com.
30. Behrouz Boochani, "This Is Manus Island. My Prison. My Torture. My Humiliation," *The Guardian* (Manchester, UK), February 18, 2016. www.theguardian.com.

31. Suzanne Degges-White, "Advocacy Begins with Connection, Listening, Understanding," *Lifetime Connections* (blog), *Psychology Today*, June 4, 2020. www.psychologytoday.com.
32. Quoted in Gray, "Forgotten Women."
33. Quoted in Karin Goodwin, "Scots Teens Who Addressed UN Committee Call on Law Makers to Involve Young People," *The National* (Glasgow, Scotland), May 12, 2019. www.thenational.scot.

Chapter Four: Risks and Rights

34. American Civil Liberties Union, "Students' Rights: Speech, Walkouts, and Other Protests," 2021. www.aclu.org.
35. American Civil Liberties Union, "Know Your Rights: Student Rights," 2021. www.aclu.org.
36. Quoted in Billy Kobin, "Louisville Christian School Expelled Student over a Rainbow Cake, Family Says," *Louisville (KY) Courier Journal*, January 14, 2020. www.courier-journal.com.
37. Quoted in Kobin, "Louisville Christian School Expelled Student over a Rainbow Cake, Family Says."
38. Quoted in American Civil Liberties Union, "Mahanoy Area School District v. B.L.," January 21, 2021. www.aclu.org.
39. Quoted in American Civil Liberties Union, "Mahanoy Area School District v. B.L."
40. Quoted in American Civil Liberties Union, "Mahanoy Area School District v. B.L."
41. National Association of Secondary School Principals, "Considerations for Principals When Students Are Planning an Organized Protest or Walkout," February 23, 2018. www.nassp.org.
42. Quoted in Samantha Schmidt, "Teens Have Been Gassed and Hit with Rubber Bullets at Protests. They Keep Coming Back," *Washington Post*, June 6, 2020. www.washingtonpost.com.
43. Quoted in Schmidt, "Teens Have Been Gassed and Hit with Rubber Bullets at Protests. They Keep Coming Back."

WHERE TO GO FOR IDEAS AND INSPIRATION

Books

Melinda Gates, *Moment of Lift: How Empowering Women Changes the World*. New York: Flatiron, 2019.

Stuart A. Kallen, *Teen Guide to Student Activism*. San Diego, CA: ReferencePoint, 2019.

Stephanie Lundquist-Arora, *How Should Society Respond to the Refugee Crisis?* San Diego, CA: ReferencePoint, 2020.

Organizations and Other Websites

American Civil Liberties Union (ACLU)
www.aclu.org

The ACLU defends individual rights and liberties specified in the Constitution. The organization's website features articles on student rights, free speech, racial justice, and information on history-making court cases. The ACLU website also provides volunteer information for teens and adults interested in promoting civil rights and liberties.

American Red Cross
www.redcross.org

Initially founded to help provide medical care for soldiers in war, the American Red Cross has a mandate to alleviate human suffering in emergencies, thereby protecting people's human right to life and safety. The Red Cross Youth link on its website provides useful information to teens about volunteer opportunities with the organization.

Amnesty International
www.amnesty.org

Amnesty International, initially founded to free prisoners of conscience, has expanded its mandate toward a broader protection of human rights since its inception in 1961. Its website offers publications of human rights issues by country or by region. It further offers information about how teens can get involved in person and/or in the Write for Rights campaign.

Human Rights Watch (HRW)
www.hrw.org

HRW is a human rights research and advocacy organization operating in over one hundred countries. Its website provides links to multiple publications on human rights topics, including women's rights, refugee rights, crisis and conflict, and torture. Its Take Action link provides teens opportunities to promote human rights on social media and through a writing campaign.

Office of the High Commissioner of Human Rights (OHCHR)
www.ohchr.org

The OHCHR is the United Nations' leading office on human rights. Its mission is to protect and promote human rights as defined in the Universal Declaration of Human Rights. Its website features publications on human rights issues in each country. The OHCHR's media center further contains speeches and commentary from its senior officials on human rights emergencies around the world.

United Nations International Children's Emergency Fund (UNICEF)
www.unicef.org

UNICEF works to defend the rights of children in over 190 countries. Its website offers research on a variety of topics concerning child welfare, including gang violence in northern Central America and annual reports on the status of the world's children. UNICEF further publishes news stories that spotlight children in the midst of humanitarian crises around the world.

Universal Declaration of Human Rights (UDHR)
www.un.org/en/universal-declaration-human-rights

The UDHR, translated into over five hundred languages, was proclaimed by the UN General Assembly in Paris on December 10, 1948, to be the common standard for universal human rights. The full-text document is available here.

News Articles
Advocates for Human Rights, "Best Practices: Using Popular Social Media Platforms for Effective Human Rights Advocacy." www.theadvocatesforhumanrights.org.

Amnesty International, "Youth, Power, Action! International Youth Strategy, 2017–2020," 2016. www.amnesty.org.

Hannah Beech et al., "Myanmar Soldiers Tell of Rohingya Slaughter," *New York Times*, September 8, 2020. www.nytimes.com.

Lucy Anna Gray, "Forgotten Women," *The Independent* (London), March 24, 2019. www.independent.co.uk.

Human Rights Watch, "An Open Prison Without End," October 8, 2020. www.hrw.org.

Joshua Rashaad McFadden, "What We Know About the Death of George Floyd in Minneapolis," *New York Times*, January 12, 2021. www.nytimes.com.

World Health Organization, "Female Genital Mutilation," February 3, 2020. www.who.int.

Vivian Yee, "Saudi Activist Who Fought for Women's Right to Drive Is Sentenced to Prison," *New York Times*, December 28, 2020. www.nytimes.com.

Documentaries/Movies

Meghna Gulzar, dir., *Chhapaak* (translated "Splash"). Mumbai, Maharashtra, India: Fox Star Studios, 2020. This is a dramatized story based on the life of Laxmi Agarwal, who survived an acid attack at age fifteen in Delhi, India, and became an advocate for survivors.

Rodd Rathjen, dir., *No Friend but the Mountains*. Australia: Aurora Films, Sweetshop & Green and Hoodlum Entertainment, 2022. This is a film adaption of Behrouz Boochani's book chronicling his harrowing journey from Iran and seven-year detention in Australia's immigration detention center on Manus Island in Papua New Guinea.

Apps

UN Human Rights Office
www.ohchr.org/EN/AboutUs/Pages/MobileApp.aspx
This free, downloadable app offers a specialized news source for human rights. It provides the user with access to human rights stories, videos from the UN Human Rights YouTube channel, as well as an optional quiz to test the user's human rights knowledge.

INDEX

Note: Boldface page numbers indicate illustrations.

acid attacks, 12–15
ActionAid, 13
Action by Christians for Abolition of Torture (ACAT-Burundi), 38
activism/advocacy
  education as first step in, 7
  raising awareness through, 18
  risks of, 50–52
Afghanistan, 19, 20–21
Agarwal, Laxmi, 13–15
Alabed, Bana, 21–22, **22**
Alford, Kimberly, 44–45
American Civil Liberties Union (ACLU), 43, 46, 56
American Red Cross, 26, 27, 56
Amnesty International, 11, 21, 22–25, 38, 56–57
Arab Spring uprisings (2011), in Syria, **10**
Assad, Bashar al-, 9
asylum seekers, 34
  detention of, 11, 34–35
  protest in support of, **35**

Barton, Clara, 27
Beattie, Michelle, 48
Benenson, Peter, 18, 23, 38
Bill of Rights, 42–43, 52
Black Lives Matter protests, **39**, 49–52
Boko Haram (jihadist movement), 4–5
Boochani, Behrouz, 33–34

Carroll, EJ, 40
cartoons
  in human rights education, 37
Chauka, Please Tell Us the Time (documentary film), 34
Chauvin, Derek, 49
Chechnya, 46
Chhanv Foundation, 14–15
Chicago Tribune (newspaper), 50
child marriages, 15–16, 36
Children for Peace, 5, 7
climate change, as human rights issue, 25
Collins, Nya, 39
Conyers, Aly, 51
Cooper, John, 39
Copeny, Mari, 29

Danforth, Paul, 48
Daughters of Eve, 17
Dear World (Alabed), 22

Degges-White, Suzanne, 35–36

education
  access to, in Niger, 36–37
  child marriage violates right to, 15
  as first step in activism, 7
  girls' access to, 19–21
Eighth Amendment, 42

Faizy, Mohib, 21
family separation policy (Trump administration), protest of, 34–35, **35**
female genital mutilation (FGM), 17–18
  advocacy against, 36–37
First Amendment, 43
Flint Kids Read campaign, 29
Floyd, George, 49
Fuller, Jade, 39

Ghabbash, Muhannad, 9–10
Girls Not Brides, 15
Green, Kennedy, 39
Greenpeace, 25
Guantanamo Bay prison, 11–12, **13**
Gupta, Anushka, 27–28

Hathloul, Loujain, al-, 29
honor killings, 16–17
human rights
  as basic freedoms/entitlements, 8
  detention of asylum seekers as violating, 11
  importance of education on, 7
Human Rights Foundation, 41
Human Rights Watch, 17, 28–30, 57

identity categories, human rights transcend, 8
India, 13–14
International Children's Peace Prize, 7
International Committee of the Red Cross (ICRC), 26–27
Iran, 11
Kadyrov, Ramzan, 46
Khoi, Mai, 41
King, Martin Luther, Jr., 30

Lambert, Katrina, 40
LEARN, 21
LGBTQ rights, 44–45
  march for, **44**
Lights for Liberty, 34
Louisville Courier Journal (newspaper), 44–45

Maloum, Divina, 5–7, **6**
Melzer, Nils, 12
Mitchell, James, 12
Mohammed, Khalid Shaikh, 12
Mohammed, Rahaf, 31–32, **32**

National Association of Secondary School Principals, 47
National, The (newspaper), 40
Niger, 15
Nkurunziza, Pierre, 38

Obama, Barack, 29, 30
Office of the High Commissioner of Human Rights (OHCHR), 57
Oumarou, Ntigang, 6–7
Owusu, Chris, 51–52

Pakistan, 16, 20, 42
    access to education in, 19–21
    acid attacks in, 13
    honor killings in, 16–17
Paty, Samuel, 37
Pew Research Center, 34
Psychology Today (magazine), 35

Red Cross, 25–28, **26**
Release Myanmar Peaceful Students campaign (Amnesty International), 24–25
Rezaiee, Mohammad Hassan, 11
Rohingya refugees, 24, 28
Rudd, Kevin, 33
Rukuki, Germain, 38

Sarvestani, Arash Kamali, 34
Saudi Arabia, 29–30, 31, 32
school walkouts
    for gun control, 47–48, **48**
    supporting LGBTQ teachers, 48–49
sex trafficking, 25
    in United States, 14
Shetty, Salil, 7
Smith, Emma Rose, 39
Smith, Mikayla, 39
social media, 23
    for group organizing, 34–35
    student rights and, 43–46
Southwell, Jacqueline, 49
students, constitutional rights of, 43
survey, on use of social media for raising awareness, 34
Syria, 21–22
    torture in, 9–10
Syrian Network for Human Rights, 10

Tepsurkayev, Salman, 46
Thomas, Zee, 39
Thunberg, Greta, 25
torture, 8
    in Chechnya, 46
    in Syrian prisons, 9–10
    US use of, 11–12
Trump administration, policy on asylum seekers, 11
Tutu, Desmond, 7

United Nations High Commissioner for Refugees (UNHCR), 4, 11, 37
United Nations International Children's Emergency Fund (UNICEF), 20, 36
United States
    process for applying for refugee sanctuary in, 32
    sex trafficking in, 14
    use of torture by government of, 11–12
Universal Declaration of Human Rights (UDHR), 8

US Constitution, 42–43
US Department of State, 14

Voice of America, 5

Wangai, Michael, 11
Wang Quanzhang, 24
waterboarding, 12
Williams, Jenni, 23–24
Women Deliver, 5

Women's March Youth Empower, 47
World Health Organization (WHO), 17
Write for Rights campaign (Amnesty International), 38

Yousafzai, Malala, 19–20, **20**, 42

Zimbabwe, 23–24

PICTURE CREDITS

Cover: John Gomez/Shutterstock.com

6: Associated Press
10: thomas koch/Shutterstock.com
13: Associated Press
16: Associated Press
20: Kyodo/Newscom
22: Associated Press
26: Associated Press
32: Associated Press
35: Jim West/agefotostock/Newscom
39: Rick3/Shutterstock.com
44: Jacob Lund/Shutterstock.com
48: Jeffrey J. Snyder/Shutterstock.com
51: Hayk_Shalunts/Shutterstock.com

ABOUT THE AUTHOR

Stephanie Lundquist-Arora has master's degrees in political science and public administration. While working on her bachelor's degree, she interned at Amnesty International, where she worked with the women's officer and trade unions officer. She has written several books for teens and children, including *How Should Society Respond to the Refugee Crisis?* When not writing, Lundquist-Arora likes traveling with her family, jogging, learning jiu-jitsu, reading, painting, and trying new foods.